THE BOUNTY

A REDEMPTION INC. NOVELLA

LAYLA REYNE

ABOUT THIS BOOK

Inspector Theodore Wagner should refuse the job offer that's too good to be true. But life has been the opposite of good for so long that when six figures and an exit from his reality are on the table, he jumps at the chance.

Catch the bounty. Take the money. Start a new life.

Except when Wags finally bags the bounty, he finds the attractive young hacker too sexy to resist. And with a target on Blaine's back, they're soon on the run from all the wrong people. But the biggest threat of all—to their safety and to Wags's new-life plan—might just be the one bed they're supposed to sleep in…together.

The Bounty is a prequel novella in the Redemption Inc. series. This M/M age-gap romantic suspense features a former spy in the middle of his mid-life crisis and the snarky, irresistible hacker he's been tasked to retrieve.

PROLOGUE

Trouble had started the moment Melissa Cruz sauntered in his direction.

He should have run. Not that it would have mattered. Runners were her business. She would have caught him eventually. Made him the offer he hadn't refused. And besides, where would he have run to, exactly? Over the glass barrier around his friends' backyard and into the wide-open canyon below? Or behind the massive Venetian dessert table at their wedding?

He should have at least tried. If he'd avoided her long enough, then maybe her need for him would have passed. Or her offer would have come later, at a time when he wasn't lonely, penniless, and wilting under the Southern California sun.

He should have steered clear altogether—of the wedding, of the bounty huntress in charge, of her assignment that had landed him in this complete and utter clusterfuck.

Disaster waiting for him on the other side of the door.

One bed and the last person he should climb into it with.

The runner he was chasing for her.

The bounty he was falling for.

ONE

Wags was born and raised in the East End. Summer swung unpredictably between sun and storms, with temps in the low- to mid-twenties Celsius, while winter was a gray, drippy affair with temps hovering just above freezing and the occasional Christmas flakes that rarely accumulated. In neither season was the weather dry, sunny, and pushing thirty-two degrees.

As he stood sweating under the San Diego sun at the Christmas-in-July wedding of his friends, Wags longed for London's dreary weather. Hell, he'd even take summer in Vienna over this. His current residence ran hotter than London in the summers but not face-of-the-sun hot. He hadn't been this hot and sweaty since his RAF days in the desert.

"You know, you can take off the coat."

Wags turned from his view of the canyon on the other side of the glass wall around Marsh and Levi's backyard to a similarly sweaty Sean Paxton, even dressed as he was in shorts and a linen shirt. Wags had seen the note on the wedding invite about informal attire, but he'd rushed straight from the station to the airport to the wedding, without a spare second or room enough in an airplane bathroom to change out of his suit.

He was paying for it now, his dress shirt soaked beneath his jacket. "No one wants to see that."

Chuckling, Sean leaned against the wall beside him, gaze drifting over the canyon. "The movies make it seem like San Diego is all sand and waves," the former FBI legat said. He'd since left the Bureau to marry his college sweethearts and run his family's commodities empire. "But really, that's only a tiny portion west of the freeway, and everything else is the desert."

A desert their mutual friend and former colleague, Marsh, wanted to live in. Who today, under the searing sun, was dressed in flannel, denim, a cowboy hat, and boots, same as his husband, Levi. "I don't know how they're not melting," Wags said with a jut of his chin toward the grooms.

Sean bumped his shoulder. "You managed in the desert, didn't you?"

"Yeah, twenty years ago."

"Well, Levi is used to this, and as for Marsh, he managed the desert too, and he grew up in hot and humid Texas."

Groaning at the thought of humidity on top of this heat, Wags held his icy glass of club soda to his forehead, and Sean laughed before taking a sip of his own drink. "How are you, Wags?"

"Been better." The past year's lowlights included a divorce, a tiny short-term flat that wasn't home, and more overtime hours than he'd ever worked, even as he anticipated getting the axe any day now. All because he'd done the right thing and helped Marsh, Levi, and Sean put away the bad guys. But at least he'd made it out of that mess alive —and sober for the first time in twenty-plus years. He held up his glass. "But getting better."

"I'm glad, Wags, and we're all glad you could make it today." Sean clasped his shoulder and gave it a squeeze, the gesture and words warm. "I'm going to go see what trouble my wife and husband are up to."

"I'm glad you're doing better too, Sean."

The former agent had always been friendly, but his gorgeous smile had never truly reached his eyes. He'd left a life and two loves behind when he'd joined the FBI, and now that he had them back and the life he'd always wanted, he was practically beaming. The fact that he'd offi-ciated the wedding of his best friend today only made his smile wider. "Thank you."

As Sean headed toward the side yard where his spouses were chatting with Marsh's son, Wags's attention was drawn in the opposite direction by Marsh's booming laugh. His friend was all smiles today, wide and bright beneath his equally wide and bright white Stetson. Wags had been attracted to the man with so much life, had harbored a raging crush on him, but seeing Marsh with Levi last summer and again today, Wags couldn't deny that there had been even more life there beneath Marsh's swaggering surface, something only Levi had been able to unlock. And though it hadn't been with him, Wags was happy to see his friend, a man he admired, so well settled.

And if Marsh could find happiness like that, if Sean could too, then maybe he…

Wags veered away from futile hopes and from the glass

wall, ambling over to the massive Venetian dessert table and plucking his third—fourth—cannoli of the day. The *click-clack* of heels on flagstone made him glance up, made him pause mid lift of the pastry as Melissa Cruz approached. He'd met the former Special Agent in Charge turned bounty hunter last summer. She was the definition of impressive…and intimidating. She was also the definition of cool, dressed in a linen pant suit, with oversize sunglasses perched in the curls piled atop her head.

"Inspector Wagner," she greeted him. "Just the man I've been looking for."

"Not much to see here." He wiped the sweat from his brow, then raked his hand through his hair, pushing back the damp, overlong strands. "Just a fortysomething man melting in the sun."

"What if I offered an escape plan?"

By the glint in her dark eyes and the one-sided tip of her lips, he didn't think she was only talking about fleeing the desert.

"What'll it cost me?"

Her smirk morphed into a smile. "I knew you were a smart man."

"Sometimes."

"An extra day in the States," she answered to his prior question. "A private flight up to cold and foggy San Francisco, and an hour of your time."

"An hour for what?"

"To entertain a job offer."

TWO

San Francisco in the summer was much more Wags's speed. Cold, dreary, and blanketed by fog. It did his British heart good and befitted the current state of his affairs.

Helping Marsh and Levi take down a transnational criminal organization last year had made him persona non grata with his employer, the Austrian Federal Police. He'd been right to cooperate with the FBI, though. They'd saved countless lives. But in doing so, they'd also ended the career of the Austrian Interior Minister and numerous others of Wags's corrupt colleagues.

The resulting scandal had also ended Wags's marriage. The writing had been on the wall for years, his and Philippe's relationship crumbling under a mountain of jealousy, secrets, and unmet expectations. But being at the center of a political shitstorm, a pariah among the upper crust where his ex liked to swim, had been the final straw.

Phil had signed the divorce papers and, once their place had sold, returned to London, leaving Wags an island unto himself in Vienna. Marsh was settled in San Diego with

Levi, and the other FBI agents he'd frequently worked with had relocated to The Hague. Sure, Wags could have returned to London too, but he'd left there for a reason; his return would not be welcomed.

So when Mel had cornered him at the wedding yesterday and offered an all-expenses-paid jaunt to San Francisco, he hadn't said no. He'd delighted, even, in emailing his boss to say he'd be in California a day longer. He half hoped there would be a termination letter waiting when he next logged in.

The glass door behind him swung open, and Mel stepped onto the balcony. "Sorry about that," she said, offering him a steaming mug of tea. "I had to scrounge around the pantry for tea bags. This business runs on coffee."

"And yet you want me to join it?"

"We're all here for redemption. Add better beverage choices to your list."

He chuckled. Tea was the least of the things he needed redemption for. He began to lower himself onto a patio chair, then hesitated. "We can go inside if it's too cold out here." She seemed dressed for the weather, in jeans and cashmere, but everyone's tolerance for gloom was different.

"Sit." She slid into the chair across from him and flitted a hand toward the inside of the flat that served as head-quarters for Redemption Inc. "Jax and Holt are in there talking hacker. Way above my pay grade."

"How is that possible? You and Brax run this place." Except her cofounder, who was also Holt's husband and Marsh's old army buddy, was conspicuously absent. "Speaking of, where is Brax, and is he okay with this plan?" He and Marsh were tight. Brax—and therefore Mel—no doubt knew about the torch Wags had carried for Marsh when they'd worked together.

Much higher than tea on his needs-redemption-for list.

"Okay, Inspector," Mel said with a knowing smirk. "Let's take those questions one at a time." She held up her index finger. "One, Brax and I trust the adults we recruit. Everyone here is competent and brings something to the table."

Before Wags even opened his mouth to ask why him, she lifted a second finger. The former SAC had a rep for being a skilled interrogator. Wags got it now; she had immediately taken command of their conversation.

"Two," she said, "Brax stayed in San Diego so the kids could have a few more days together." That tracked with what Wags observed at the wedding. Brax and Holt's daughter had been attached at the hip to Marsh and Levi's son, the two of them inseparable.

"And three." She lifted a third finger, this one adorned with a giant yellow diamond, courtesy of her husband being the CEO of his family's shipping company. "Yes, Brax agreed to this plan. We need someone on the team with connections in European law enforcement."

"Because you can't technically hunt bounties in Europe."

"Technically." Her earlier smirk returned. She'd clearly skirted that technicality before. "Especially now that we're a licensed organization."

Ah, so she needed someone else to do the skirting. "So it's my arse on the line."

She didn't correct him. "Marsh speaks highly of you. Says you have the connections we need. And you've proven you'll fight for the good guys." She reached into her pocket, withdrew a folded slip of paper, and held it out to him. "Your reputation and track record are worth something. Your arse too."

Her terrible Cockney accent made him laugh. The number written on the scrap of paper almost made him drop his mug. "This would be the annual?"

"No. That's for the current job. You complete it, bring back the runner, and we'll discuss annual pay and benefits."

He sipped his tea, eyes glued to the six-figure amount that was more than any annual salary he'd ever been paid. And for only one job. If he did it well, there would be more, including benefits. All while working for the good guys, unlike the folks back…not home.

He folded the paper and lifted his gaze, meeting the sparkling brown one across from him. She knew she had him. No sense pretending otherwise. "What do you need me to do?"

THREE

Only one job.

That one job was going on twenty-eight days now and had included stops clear across Europe, all to end up in the most horribly predictable place possible.

Vienna.

At one of Wags's favorite pubs, no less.

He should have just parked his arse here to start and waited for the bounty to come to him. He'd put out the call to his connections, bartenders included, and Ernie, who owned this particular pub near Vienna's city center, had called him yesterday about a person fitting his bounty's description. Sure enough, as Wags slid onto the stool behind a waiting seltzer and lime, he spied his target in the adjoining game room, shooting pool with a couple of guys, tourists if the maroon West Ham kits they wore were any indication.

Wags had to hand it to the kid. He'd covered his tracks well, using his forgery skills and stash of cryptocurrency to stay a step ahead of Wags and the other law enforcement agencies—and criminals—after him. So why risk exposure now? Did he think himself far enough ahead? Granted, he'd used fake papers to enter the country, but neither he nor exhaustion had changed his appearance much. Long, dark top strands that fell over the shaved sides of his head, kohl-lined eyes, a scruffy beard, and painted nails. Even shy of six feet, he stood out, and Austria was the second most likely place where someone would recognize Blaine Anthony.

He was the son of a once powerful US congressman, Stewart Anthony, who'd been a presidential hopeful and surrogate son to the late Charles Sanders, an Austrian trafficker in philanthropist's clothing and the head of the criminal organization Wags had helped Marsh and Levi take down. With Blaine's help. Blaine was supposed to be in protective custody pending the conclusion of his father's prolonged circus of a trial and pending his own sentencing for fraud and digital forgery, but he'd slipped his leash a month ago.

"That your boy?" Ernie asked, his Aussie brogue thick, as he slid a steaming-hot Scotch egg and basket of golden-brown chips in front of him.

He dipped one of the crinkle-cut potatoes into the ramekin of ranch—bless the Americans, and bless Ernie for his Aussie, British, American mashup of a pub—and popped it into his mouth. "That's him. He showed up yesterday?"

Ernie nodded. "Hustled a couple of regulars last night. Targeting the tourists tonight," he said, the good humor fading from his brogue. He rested his forearms on the bar top, leaning closer and lowering his voice. "Would appreciate you getting him outta here before more serious trouble follows."

Meaning Ernie knew exactly who he was, even if the tourists didn't.

Wags picked up one half of the egg. "Let me just savor this taste of ho—"

Raised voices in a dialect he knew well carried from the game room, the tourists tossing their cues onto the pool table and crowding into Blaine's space, reaching for the wad of bills Blaine had snatched off the rail. Wags cursed. The last thing any of them needed was for Blaine to draw more attention. Regretfully surrendering the piping-hot egg, Wags snagged another chip from the basket before sliding off his stool. He skirted the edge of the dance floor, then weaved through the audience gathering to witness a potential brawl.

Wags couldn't let that happen.

Taking a gamble and channeling every bit of Marsh he could muster, he covered his Cockney with a Texas drawl and sidled beside Blaine, throwing an arm over his shoulders and eyeing the two Hammer fans. "There a problem here?"

"Your son hustled us," the more brutish of the two East Londoners spat.

Wags opened his mouth to try and deescalate the situation, but Blaine swerved in a different direction, snaking an arm around his waist and nestling closer against his side. "Not my dad."

The implication was clear, and the shock that painted the tourists' faces was priceless. Would have made Wags laugh in any other circumstance. Almost made him cheer in this case when the two strangers took a step back. Wanting another of those, Wags kissed the side of Blaine's head, playing along with his ruse. "Did you hustle them, baby?"

Blaine's shrug was pure rich-kid insolence, and the brutish one's fist clenched. Wags needed to end this now.

He kept an arm around Blaine but dropped the fake accent, unfurling his real one. "I'd think a couple of guys from the East End would know better."

The brutish one blanched, but the tall, skinny one lifted his chin. "Doesn't change the fact that he hustled us."

"For how much?"

"Five hundred euros."

Wags caught the *nice job* that was on the tip of his tongue, opting instead for diplomacy. "You should have known better," he reiterated to the Hammers, then to Blaine, "And you shouldn't have gone so high. Give 'em back two-fifty."

Neither party looked happy, but they'd avoided a brawl. Blaine handed back half the money, and the onlookers dispersed. With his arm still over Blaine's shoulders, Wags directed him toward the back exit. "Let's get out of here."

Once they were in the alley behind the pub, the door slamming shut behind them, Blaine surprised him again, maneuvering around to his front and dropping his voice several octaves. "So what do I owe you for that?" He gazed up at him with dark, bloodshot eyes. "A little hand action? A blowjob?"

Heat and awareness exploded between them, and Wags rocked back on his heels. He wasn't blind. Blaine was an attractive man, compact and leanly muscled, with a firm arse that Wags had most certainly not noticed when he'd been bent over that pool table. Like he also hadn't noticed the exposed strip of smooth, pale skin between the waistband of his jeans and the hem of his hoodie. Because Blaine was his target, a case file. And Blaine had absolutely zero idea who he was. Risky on all counts. Riskier even than the tourists he'd just run off. "Maybe I rescued you out of the goodness of my heart."

"Don't," Blaine said. "I tried that. Never works out." He closed the distance between them, forcing Wags back a step, then another, until his back hit the wall. "So back to my original question…" He flattened his palms on Wags's abs and coasted them up his torso, fingertips under the lapels of his denim jacket, hands spreading closer to his nipples—and fuck, if he teased them, Wags would have no hope of not rutting forward. There'd been no one since he and Philippe had separated. His body—his cock, more precisely—was fighting his brain for control of this situation. Take Blaine up on his tempting offer, or do the right thing and take him into custody. Get him to safety.

Blaine pressing his hard body along his, the impressive length of his cock against Wags's hip, was not helping. Wags bit his bottom lip, libido racing. Fuck, what a young man with stamina could do with a piece like that. How it would fill his mouth, heavy on his tongue. How hard and long he could fuck him with it. And what the hell did a young man like Blaine see in a washed-up, middle-aged divorcé like him?

His mind latched on to that last question, to those undeniable facts, and he forced out the words he needed to say to defuse the escalating heat between them. "We shouldn't. I'm fifteen years older than you, and—"

Blaine rocked his hips forward. "That doesn't—" He froze, eyes growing wide. "Wait, how do you know how old I am?"

"Blaine…" His eyes grew wider still, and Wags realized his slip. Two pieces of information—age and name—a stranger wouldn't know. "Shit."

And the runner was off again, ripping out of his arms and toward the street. He barely made it a few steps, though, before two men appeared from around the corner, blocking his exit. Distinctly not tourists. Big and muscled, with tattoos on their knuckles and weapons in harnesses beneath their coats.

Cursing, Blaine spun back in Wags's direction and did the last thing Wags expected, pinning him against the wall again and craning up so his lips brushed his cheek, his whisper hot in Wags's ear. "Can you protect me from them too?"

And then Blaine's lips were on his. Chapped and warm, firm and demanding, forcing Wags to open for his tongue that swept inside, tangling with his in a groan-inducing kiss that Wags ached to drown in. Like he ached to run his hands all over Blaine's body, to bury his face between those firm cheeks he'd most certainly noticed, to ride his arse and spill his come all over it.

"Now they won't suspect you," Blaine whispered against his lips before ending the fantasy and ripping himself out of Wags's arms again. He darted back inside the bar, leaving Wags a lust-fueled mess.

Alone in the alley, facing down the pair of advancing thugs.

But as lust-dazed as Wags was, he realized what Blaine had just done for him. Provided cover. So when he swaggered into the way of the two men, he played it up like he'd done inside with the tourists, pretending to be drunk and left hanging. Not a stretch, his erection fighting a war with his jeans. "I didn't even get his name..." Pouting, he fell back against the door and stroked his cock, going for more shock value.

And just like with the tourists inside, he got the reaction he wanted. The thugs rolled their eyes and turned on their heels, exiting the alley and rounding the corner toward the front of the pub.

"No use!" he called out. After twenty-eight days, he knew the drill. Blaine was long gone. And this time, Wags had been the one who helped him escape. He rested his head back against the door and closed his eyes. "Fuck."

FOUR

Wags sank to his knees, not giving a damn about his aching joints, not arsed at all that his last pair of clean jeans was about to be ruined inside and out. All that mattered were the dark, hooded eyes gazing down at him, the plump cock hanging out of Blaine's unzipped jeans, the black-painted nails scraping across his scalp as Blaine yanked him forward with a grunt. Wags closed his eyes and parted his lips, hungry for the hot, silky steel gliding across his tongue, the salty precome flooding his senses, the moans ringing in his ears.

Ringing…

Not a moan.

A trilling chime.

Fuck.

Wags threw out an arm, silencing the bad ringing while Blaine's moans continued in his drowsy head. His own joining the chorus as he curled his fingers around his stiff cock, jerking himself as he'd done countless times since Friday. He fondled his balls with his other hand, imagining they were Blaine's, heavy in his hand like his cock on his tongue.

He shuttled his fist faster, harder, in time with Fantasy Blaine's jutting hips, shoving his cock down Wags's throat, gagging him.

Stealing his breath and another sleepless night.

Fucking his mouth.

Fucking his arse.

He flipped himself over and shoved a pillow between his legs, groaning at the blessed friction. Shoved three slick fingers between his lips and sucked, imagining it was Blaine he tasted, Blaine fucking him into the mattress, Blaine shouting with him as they came together.

The trilling resumed.

He silenced the alarm once more, but before he could toss the phone back onto the nightstand, the device vibrated in his hand.

He squinted at the text.

Marsh: See you in 20.

Twenty?

Wags had set his alarm so he'd have an hour and a half before their call. He was halfway to replying a *fuck off with your early cowboy nonsense* when the rest of the lust fog cleared. He must've pressed the Snooze button more than once without realizing.

"Fuck you," he cursed to no one, then peeled himself off the sticky sheets and hauled himself to the shower, reality a far cry from fantasy.

FIVE

Wags hustled out of the en-suite bathroom, steam licking his heels as he darted across the guest room to his trilling computer. He answered the call, video off. "Give me a minute."

"You, Theodore George Wagner, are the one who called this meeting." Marsh's grumbled full-naming him was belied by his devilish smirk. "At nine o'clock on a school night."

"It's still summer break," Wags grumbled back as he scrounged in his duffel for jeans and a shirt. "School's not back in session there for another couple of weeks, and from what David told me at the wedding, he should be in Texas until then, helping your moms on the ranch."

"He's got you there," Jax said, the Redemption Inc. hacker appearing in another box onscreen. Their mohawk was no longer dyed red and white as it had been for the Christmas-in-July wedding, but rather bright-orange and black, the local baseball team's colors, if Wags recalled correctly.

Marsh waved that off. "Beside the point. I want to know why the good inspector is late for his own meeting."

"Not an inspector anymore." The termination letter he'd hoped for had in fact arrived ten minutes after he'd left Redemption Inc. HQ. He'd celebrated that night with an overpriced steak and loaded baked potato, all very American. A month and no bounty later, he worried he might have celebrated too soon. Hence the call he'd scheduled with the American cavalry. "Look, it's six in the morning here, and I just got out of the shower, so unless you want to see me naked…"

Marsh reclined in his chair and removed his reading glasses, tossing them on his desk and pinching the bridge of his nose. "I'll pass, thanks. Go get dressed."

A year ago, the casual dismissal by one of the hottest men he'd ever met would've stung. Hell, a month ago, it probably still would have smarted, even though Wags was genuinely happy for his friend who'd found love. But after Friday night in the alley, after the past two days of jerking off to the memory of Blaine's tongue down his throat, of Blaine's hard body rutting against his, and after how hard he'd come this morning to the fantasy of where that night might have led, Wags just chuckled.

Dressed, he slid into the chair behind his laptop and turned on his camera.

Marsh winced.

"That bad?" Wags said, raking a hand through his wet hair and pushing the overlong strands out of his face.

"You look like hell, Wags."

"Well, let's see… I've been from Dublin to Istanbul and back again with a dozen stops in between, only to end up in Vienna, of all fucking places."

"But hey, at least Sean's penthouse is nice."

Nice was an understatement. He glanced out the balcony doors of the Old Town penthouse and spied the Stephansdom towers piercing the colorful morning sky. If Philippe knew he was staying here, he'd probably burn those divorce papers. "Tell Sean I said thanks."

The last box onscreen flickered to life, Brax appearing with a sleeping auburn-haired child sprawled across his chest. "Sorry I'm late," he said, his hazel gaze straying adoringly to his daughter. "Someone decided she had to sleep right here." He ran a hand over her back, and when Lily didn't budge, he lifted his gaze back to the screen. "So Blaine is in Vienna?"

Wags nodded. "As of last Thursday. Maybe longer. One of my contacts sent up a flare, and I hopped on the train from Munich, where we'd last sighted him."

"You made contact?"

You could say that…

"Friday night. I didn't get a chance to introduce myself before two Bratva goons scared him off."

Marsh leaned forward and propped his elbows on his desk. "To where this time?" He had a vested interest in making sure Blaine made it back to the States in time to testify against his father. His firsthand account of Stewart's illegal activities would all but seal the case against the former congressman.

"Can't say for certain, but none of his known aliases have left the country, and none of my sources are reporting him elsewhere either."

"Same on our end," Jax added. "No surveillance of him anywhere."

"Do we know why he's in Vienna?" Brax asked.

While Wags hadn't been able to find Blaine again, he had found a reason for his presence, that thing that had lured him to the very place he shouldn't be. "There's an auction in Old Town later today. I sent Jax the details last night. It's off-book, no names listed, but word is, there are several one-of-a-kind Pinclers in the auction lot."

Marsh straightened in his chair. "That's gotta be it." The handcrafted chess boxes had played a key role in bringing down Charles and Stewart.

"Catherine confirmed," Jax said. Catherine, Charles's granddaughter, had eventually turned state's evidence, and they could consult with her when items such as these made an appearance. "I was able to cobble together a tentative lot list. I'm pushing that through to the encrypted chat now. The rest of the items are from the Sanders estate in Salzburg."

Wags opened the encrypted document, scratching his scruffy jaw as he scanned the list. Nothing jumped out on his first read-through, but on his second pass, he noticed the item out of place among the other treasures at the same time as Marsh, both of them declaring, "The diary."

"In Japanese," Wags added, noting the crucial fact. "Blaine's mother's?"

"If I had to guess," Marsh agreed with a nod. "Claudia Anthony's father was from Japan. She was fluent. Blaine is too."

"So let's assume Blaine is after his mother's diary. Sentimental value or…"

"*Or*," Marsh stressed. "Blaine wants to put his father away for good. When Levi and I questioned him last year, he implied his father had something to do with Claudia's death. That he'd threatened to do the same to Blaine if he didn't toe the line."

"But hasn't Stewart implied the opposite?" Brax said. "That struggles with Blaine at home drove Claudia to suicide?"

Marsh side-eyed his best friend. "I know which Anthony I believe."

Wags agreed. "Blaine must think there's proof of his father's guilt in that diary."

"Couldn't he just forge it?" Jax said. "It's what he does—and he does it incredibly well."

"He probably wants it for sentimental value too," Marsh said. "We got the impression he and Claudia were close."

A united front against his father, until Stewart had silenced one of them and used it to deter the other. And Wags had thought his father was an arsehole for cutting him off and throwing him out for being gay. But in no scenario could he imagine his father, as awful as he was, going as far as murder or blackmail.

"Do we think he'll turn himself in once he has the diary?" Brax asked.

"He went willingly into custody before," Marsh said. "And stayed there."

"Until he didn't," Wags said, "otherwise I wouldn't have been traipsing across Europe for the past month."

"That's not on us," Brax said at the same time as Marsh's, "He bribed one of the custodial officers with bitcoin and a blowjob."

Wags's stomach flipped, his nighttime fantasy twisting and contorting into something darker. Was he just another mark? Had Blaine simply been doing what he usually did? Bribing and flirting his way to freedom?

"He wants out of this mess," Marsh said, drawing Wags's attention back to him. "Then he wants to move on."

"Move on to what?" Wags asked.

When silence greeted him, the last piece of the puzzle fell into place. "He's not just a bounty, is he? He's a prospective asset for Redemption Inc."

"We all have a vested interest in bringing Blaine home," Brax said. "Safe and sound."

SIX

Wags stepped out of the elevator into the building's lobby, tugging at the lapels of his borrowed suit jacket. He was certain he'd never donned threads this fine before, but Sean's suits were clearly tailored just for him, including a slim fit around the middle that was doing Wags no favors. He wasn't out of shape, per se, but the past month of globe-trotting hadn't exactly lent itself to balanced meals and regular exercise. Hadn't lent itself to regular shaves either. The coat was tight, his clean cheeks pale, his neck being strangled by a tie for the first time in weeks, but at least he looked the part. And maybe a little less familiar to those at the auction who might otherwise recognize him.

"Mr. Wagner?" He spun on his heel and found the uniformed concierge holding up a manila envelope. "This was dropped off for you."

"Thank you," he said, accepting the package, and then, seeing no car at the curb, he meandered to the seating area by the windows. He emptied the contents of the envelope onto the side table: a burner phone—why? Redemption had an encrypted channel—and an American passport with his picture, the name Parker Barrow, and an address in Rowena, Texas. Suppressing his irritation, he focused instead on the passport's pages, examining the holograms and stamps. It was top-notch work.

He pulled out his regular phone and texted Jax via the encrypted channel. **Nice work on the passport, but Bonnie and Clyde? Really?** Bonnie Parker and Clyde Barrow, American bandits known for robbery and murder. From Texas, no less, meaning he'd have to use that damn accent tonight. This could only be one person's doing. **Marsh can fuck right off. And why do I need a burner?**

His phone rang, Jax's name lighting up the screen. He lifted the phone to his ear, ready to curse Marsh out some more, but Jax didn't give him a chance, asking abruptly, "Where did you get the passport and phone?"

"A package was waiting for me at the concierge desk in Sean's building."

"The German passports we had made for you and Blaine are in the car coming to pick you up. ETA two minutes."

He stood and gathered his now mysterious items. "Suppose you didn't leave this other phone, then, either?"

"Why? We're on an encrypted channel."

Exactly, so then who— His mind rewound to Friday night at the pub, to the accent he'd used when he'd first approached Blaine and the two men he'd hustled. He examined the passport again. It wasn't just nice work; it was flawless. He powered on the burner. One app—a cryptocurrency exchange; no saved contacts; one number in the call history—San Diego area code.

"Hold a second," he said to Jax, then walked back the

concierge desk. "Ma'am, did you happen to catch the name of the person who delivered that package for me?"

"Deniz Aslan," she said with a smile. "He's a popular courier here in Old Town."

"Not one of ours," Jax said, having overheard the exchange. "Car's arriving. Black Benz."

"Thank you," Wags told the concierge, then exited the building.

"I'll find Aslan," Jax said. "Determine who hired him."

"No need. I know who it was." The car idled at the curb, and he slid into the back seat, where another manila envelope waited with no doubt nice but not flawless passports. "I'll keep you posted."

Hanging up on their protests, he waited for the car to pull into traffic before dialing the one number on the burner. The call connected on the first ring.

"Inspector Wagner," Blaine greeted him with a smirk Wags could hear in his voice.

That made Wags's own lips twitch. "You know who I am."

"You're not the only one with hacker friends. Though I guess you're just Theodore now."

He slumped in the seat, reveling in Blaine's crisp, unaccented voice, in the banter he missed almost as much as Blaine's lips and body. They hadn't been in each other's company long, but those few minutes were enough to light a spark. "Most people call me Wags. Or Teddy."

"But you sound more like a Theodore."

"How's that?"

"You're all British and shit."

Wags laughed, for real, for the first time in he couldn't remember how long, and warmth spread through his chest.

Into Blaine's voice too. "Okay, maybe Teddy, then." Grew hotter as he hummed low in Wags's ear. "Your laugh is warm and soft, like a teddy." He groaned, and the words were out of Wags's mouth before he could catch them.

"What are you doing?"

A gasp. "Stroking my dick." A grunt. "Imagining all that warmth and softness clenching around me."

Wags bit his bottom lip and willed his cock not to get any ideas. "I know your game. You flirt to get your way."

"Did that feel like a game to you the other night?" Blaine's voice sank another octave, grew quiet, like they were sharing a secret. "How many times have you jerked off since Friday? I've lost count. My dick won't quit. Every time I think about shoving inside you… Would you let me, Teddy?"

Wags's hole clenched, and he spread his legs, making room for his stiffening cock, even as he warned, "Now's not the time."

The sexy laugh that rumbled over the line didn't help. "Not a no."

Wags ran his hand down his torso, halfway to his cock, on the cusp of losing the battle against jerking off in the back seat of a hired car, but at the last second flailed for a distraction, his hand landing instead on the passports beside him. "So now I have two forms of identification."

"Mine's better."

"Of course it is, but what if someone recognizes me?"

"That's a risk no matter what fake ID you use. Hopefully you shaved."

Wags chuckled. "I did." He palmed his too-smooth jaw, then picked up the passport Blaine had made him. "What do you want clean-shaven Parker Barrow to do tonight?"

"Win me back my mother's diary."

Good. Blaine trusted him, at least enough to handle being in the line of fire for him. "How much am I authorized to bid?"

"Five million US dollars."

Wags whistled low. "Forgery is a profitable business."

"Judging by that deposit you made recently, so is bounty hunting. Good thing too. You didn't have much left."

"No, I didn't," he admitted. No use lying. Blaine had clearly seen his account's balance. And as the car neared their destination, there were other particulars they needed to sort, including his conflicting missions. "I'm not supposed to be at this event to participate," he told Blaine.

"What was your role?"

"To observe, then bring you in."

"You'll do the second."

Wags leaned forward in his seat, eyeing the line of cars dropping off folks in impossibly finer threads than the ones he wore. "And the first?"

"Leave that to me."

He straightened. "How?"

"I'll get in touch with Jax. You just get me that diary."

SEVEN

"Four-point-seven-five," the auctioneer repeated from the pulpit, and as Wags lowered his paddle for the umpteenth time in less than ten minutes, he worried his pounding heart would beat out of his chest.

Four million, 750 thousand US dollars.

Phil was an interior designer. Wags had accompanied his ex to estate auctions before, but no bid for staging furniture had ever come close to the amounts being offered for Claudia Anthony's diary.

And no estate sale they'd attended had ever been this dangerous.

Wags sat alone on a pew in one of Vienna's oldest churches, a small Romanesque structure in Old Town. Scattered among the other pews were mobsters, mercs, and dirty politicians. Associates of Charles's that Wags recognized from case files. One of Catherine's minions, a snooty French woman he'd questioned last year. An abhorrent American television news personality who, Wags assumed, was there on Stewart's behalf. High-ranking officials in the

Austrian government. Representatives from the triads, the Yakuza, and the Sicilian Mafia. And on the pew across the aisle from Wags, the two Bratva soldiers from Friday night sat on either side of an older gentleman with salt-and-pepper hair and a younger woman in a form-fitting black dress, her knee-high leather boots as shiny as her fall of glossy black hair.

All of them knew who he was, Wags was certain, and the inherent danger fueled the adrenaline coursing through his veins. It had been years since he'd felt this alive, and as Catherine's stand-in raised her paddle again—4.8 million—the stakes ratcheted higher.

And higher again, the Russians bidding 4.9.

Before Wags could even lift his paddle, the American beat him to Blaine's max—five million.

Which was eclipsed the next second by the Russians going to 5.5.

"Fuck," Wags cursed under his breath. He yanked the burner out of his pocket, preparing to text Blaine, when the phone vibrated in his hand, a message appearing in the chat they'd started earlier.

10mil end this now

He shot his paddle into the air before he could second-guess himself or Blaine. "Ten million."

Gasps echoed around the room, and the elder Russian leaned forward, glancing around his guard, his dark-blue eyes narrowed. Wags held his stare, meeting the challenge, blood whooshing in his ears, until the older man conceded with a nod. Smiling, the Russian straightened and laid a hand over the woman's, holding her paddle down.

They were out. And so was everyone else. Thank fuck.

"Going once, going twice," said the auctioneer, before announcing, "Sold to Mr. Barrow."

Wags's sigh of relief was interrupted by the auctioneer's assistant appearing at the end of his pew. "Will you be bidding on anything else, sir?"

Wags shook his head. "Think I've spent enough," he told the assistant, affecting the Texas drawl to match his ID.

The frazzled assistant cracked a smile. Another win. "Follow me, please."

As they moved toward the front of the nave, to the antechamber door where each prior winner had been led, Wags walked with the swagger of his confident Texan friend, playing the part, while curious and hostile stares drilled into his back. They knew who he was, but not whom he worked for. Did they suspect? The Bratva surely did after what they'd witnessed the other night. Would they follow him once he stepped outside? Would any of the other bidders? Where was he even supposed to go? Blaine hadn't covered next steps in his texts. Because he hadn't expected him to win? Or because he'd left him to the wolves?

Except the funds were there—ten million—when Wags went to transfer them, meaning Blaine hadn't abandoned him completely. He kept waiting for the burner to vibrate as he finished the transaction and collected Claudia's diary, but it remained obnoxiously silent. He texted Blaine as he navigated the church's narrow hallways. **I'm headed to the penthouse unless you tell me otherwise.**

A hand shot out of an open doorway, grabbing him by the biceps and yanking him inside a shadowed room. The door slammed shut behind him, and Wags drew back his right arm, ready to swing.

"It's me, Teddy." Hands up, palms out, Blaine shifted into the colorful prism cast by the room's stained-glass windows. He was dressed the same as the other night—jeans, T-shirt, hoodie—and his eyes shone with the same gleam they had then. The thrill of the game, of the win, and shining even brighter now as they alighted on the diary in Wags's other hand. "Is that it?"

He handed the diary to Blaine, who held it reverently, thumbs skimming over the soft leather cover embossed with a chrysanthemum. A hard swallow later, he crossed the room to the cluttered desk, where a backpack lay in the halo of the lamp there. He examined the diary more clinically, checking its cover and spine and fanning the pages. Seemingly satisfied, he tucked the diary inside the bag, then rested back against the edge of the desk. When he lifted his gaze to Wags, it was dark and hooded, heated, and his usually sharp voice gravelly. "Come here."

"We need—"

He crooked a finger. "Come here, Teddy."

As if drawn by a magnet, Wags closed the distance, moving into the space between Blaine's spread legs. Blaine grabbed his belt buckle and yanked him closer. So close that Wags could feel the heat of his breath through the thin material of his dress shirt.

"That was so fucking hot." Blaine glided his hands over Wags's hips to his behind, clasping his cheeks and hauling him closer still, molding them together. His lips brushed the underside of Wags's chin, making Wags tremble with want. "I'm gonna blow you right here in this church office."

Wags's cock stiffened. All that adrenaline from earlier was spinning his libido higher and higher, but here wasn't safe. "We need to get out of here."

"It won't take long." Blaine deftly unbuckled his belt while torturing Wags with his lips and tongue, kissing a path from behind his ear to his collar. "How do you want me to do it, Teddy? Easy or rough?"

Blaine slipped a hand inside his pants, cupping him through his boxers, and Wags melted. "Rough," he confessed on a groan. "Sloppy." He didn't want perfect. He wanted passionate, alive, too needy to be neat.

"Fuck, I knew you were hung, but this…" He stroked him, rough and hard, exactly the way Wags ached for it. "I can't wait to get my lips around you. Make a complete mess of your cock, your balls, your hole."

"Bloody hell, I need…" All those things. He tunneled his fingers through Blaine's top strands, eager to push him down and hold on tight. But the last sliver of his rational brain tried to convince him otherwise, to protect the man promising to take him apart. "Blaine, we need to—"

The *rat-a-tat-tat* of gunfire rattled the stained-glass windows, and on its heels, an explosion shook the walls.

Wags ripped himself out of Blaine's arms and wrenched up his pants. "We need to go!" He grabbed Blaine's bag with one hand, Blaine's hand with the other, and bolted for the door, listening for a break in the commotion outside, for an opening to escape.

Blaine's hand clenched around his, and Wags glanced over his shoulder, taking in the younger man's wide eyes and paler-than-usual complexion. He was terrified. Wags tugged him closer, handed him his bag, and brushed a kiss across his forehead. "I've got you. Trust me."

Dark eyes gazed up at him with the kind of faith Wags had long forgotten. "I do."

Footsteps thundered past their door, headed toward the

main part of the church. Followed by silence. He cracked open the door.

"Careful," Blaine hissed behind him, his grip on Wags's hand nearly cutting off his circulation.

Wags waited another couple of seconds before poking his head out the door and glancing both ways. Shouts from the left, the direction of the chapel. To the right, an open door under the blue-and-white Ausfahrt sign.

"Follow me," he told Blaine, then without giving him time to object, tugged him out into the hallway and toward the exit.

They were a foot away from freedom when one of the Sicilians appeared in the doorway. Wags didn't think, just acted, grabbing the open glass door and slamming it into the man's face. The mobster got his hands up in time to protect his face, but the shattering glass around him froze him in place long enough for Wags and Blaine to slip by.

And come face-to-face with his partner.

The second Sicilian lifted a pistol, and Wags dove for his side, shoving him back and his gun arm up, the shot going awry as they stumbled backward.

Enough of a window for Blaine to escape. "Run!" Wags shouted. "Get out of here!"

"I'm not leaving you!"

Now we wanted to be caught. Wanted to help too, scrambling behind the mobster and kicking his knees out from under him, upsetting everyone's balance and sending them all down together.

"You can't run," the Sicilian said in accented English, letting go of his pistol and grabbing Blaine's ankle. "Give me the diary, and you can go."

"We're not gonna do that," Wags said, getting his feet

back under him and his hands under the mobster's collar, hauling him back and wrestling him to the side.

Righting himself, Wags grabbed Blaine's hand, yanked him up, and turned—into Mr. Shattered Glass. He was bloody, and angry, judging by his hardened dark eyes, and more shouts and footsteps were approaching from inside. Wags worried for a moment how he was going to get them out of this.

Worry that ratcheted higher when gunfire popped behind them. He curved over Blaine, bending them at the waist, anticipating impact.

Only for the Sicilian to fall at their feet.

Wags whipped his gaze over Blaine's head.

"Get out of here," the elder Russian said from where he stood behind the woman with a still smoking gun. "We'll cover you."

As much as the detective in Wags wanted to ask why, the protector in him demanded otherwise. He nodded his thanks to their unlikely saviors, and then, arm still around Blaine, got them the hell out of there.

EIGHT

Wags leaned against the sink in the tiny hotel bathroom, phone to his ear, trying to speak quietly while still talking loud enough to be heard over the planes from the airport next door.

He and Blaine had escaped the church in Vienna, using the cover provided by the Russians to make a mad dash to the U-Bahn. They'd caught a train to the nearest rail station, then hopped on the direct express to Bratislava.

"Your ride is en route," Mel said. "The plane was already in New York. It'll arrive there tomorrow morning at eight and depart again at eight thirty."

Wags pulled the phone from his ear and glanced at the time.

Nine hours from now. Nine long hours to keep Blaine safe. Nine even longer hours to keep his hands to himself. That look of fear in Blaine's eyes at the church, the faith he'd put in Wags... He couldn't abuse that trust, couldn't take advantage.

"Did you get an ID on the bidders?" he asked Mel,

distracting himself with the mundane. "The ones I didn't know."

Blaine had passed out against his shoulder not long after the train had left the station. Once the conductor had come through to check their tickets and passports, the Redemption fakes coming in handy, Wags had debriefed with Jax over their encrypted chat, getting down all the details he could while his memory was still fresh.

"We did," Mel said. "Between your and Blaine's accounts, all the players were identified."

"The Russians?"

"Ours."

He shot off the sink. "*Yours?*" And promptly ran into the opposite wall—definitely not enough room in the tiny space to vent his surprise.

"In a manner of speaking."

"So Friday night..."

"They were acting independently then. They weren't today."

"Good God, woman, what kind of juice do you have?"

"The good stuff, Mr. Wagner." And if she was tilting a glass of the very best champagne to her lips just then, Wags wouldn't have been surprised. "I understand we have the diary."

"We do."

"And what does it say about Stewart Anthony?"

"I don't know." He pictured her lowering that glass and mentally cheered. "I thought it right to give Blaine some time with it first."

"Fair enough." The smile in her voice made him regret his momentary spite, and the tension he hadn't realized he'd been carrying in his shoulders began to dissipate. He'd spent so long watching his back, working for people he didn't trust, that the concept of folks using their power to eliminate threats to him, to do good, would take some getting used to.

"I'm sorry," he said. "It's been a long day."

"A long month, Mr. Wagner. You've done well. Get some rest, then be at the airport with Blaine and that diary tomorrow morning. We'll get you home."

Ending the call, he leaned against the door and closed his eyes, fixating on that one word.

Home.

What did she mean by it? Dropping him back in Vienna or London, then on to the States for Blaine? Or was he riding along to the States with Blaine and then back to Europe? Could it be that she was offering him more? A different, better home. Could he have that? Had he done well enough to make this a permanent gig? Did he want that? Salary and benefits, coworkers he could trust, a place to call his own when he wasn't traveling? Yes to all that, plus Blaine in his be— He shook off the thought before it fully formed, pushing off the door and pacing the two short steps the room allowed.

He braced his hands on the sink and stared at the man in the mirror. All forty-plus years of battle—his family, his marriage, his years of military service, his years with the Austrian Federal Police, his decades at the bottom of a bottle before he'd sobered up—all of it etched into the wrinkles on his face, painted in the strands of silvering blond hair, folded into his weary soul. He wasn't a catch. He was a heavy anchor, as dangerous to Blaine as any of the people chasing them, even if Blaine didn't see that. Hell, Wags could only see it himself like this, standing alone in the dim reality, outside the blinding light of the attraction between them, away from the adrenaline that had made things brighter.

He turned on the cold tap, cupped his hands under the faucet, and splashed chilly water on his face. He would go out there and be professional. Secure the bounty and the diary, catch some half-aware shut-eye in the corner chair, then get them to the airport on time in the morning.

Get them home.

He had enough to redeem himself for already without adding to the list another moment of weakness, of self-ishness.

He dried his hands and opened the door.

Blaine sat cross-legged in the middle of the king-size bed, chin wobbling, tears streaming down his pale cheeks. He lifted his face, dark eyes full of anger-drenched despair. "He did it. My father really did it." He choked on a sob. "And I did nothing to stop it."

Wags's best intentions took a hurtling jump out the window. He climbed onto the bed beside Blaine and curled an arm around his shoulders. "You were just a kid."

"I was twenty."

"And just as much a pawn to him as your mother was. As all of us were."

Blaine gestured helplessly with the diary, lifting it weakly, then letting it fall to his knee. "She was trying to protect me. She was going to get us out. He couldn't..." He swallowed hard and forced out scratchy words. "He couldn't have that and be president."

Couldn't be president at all after the long list of heinous crimes he'd committed had finally come to light. And now there would be another crime added to that list, foretold in the victim's own words, held in the care of another of Stewart's victims. "How did Charles get hold of the diary?"

Blaine picked up the journal again and flipped to the last page, holding it open for Wags to read the short, devastating note.

Charles, I know. Stewart knows I know and will kill me for it. Protect my son when I'm gone. —C

Wags's stomach lurched, his heart with it, tumbled by sorrow for the life lost and the one left behind. "Oh, baby." He gathered Blaine the rest of the way into his arms. "I'm so sorry."

Blaine's sobs broke free, the book slipping from his grasp as his body shook, as he burrowed deeper into the embrace, his tears soaking Wags's shirt. Wags couldn't help wondering if this was the first time Blaine had truly let himself grieve. For his mother, for himself, for the life and family he should have had. He carded his fingers through Blaine's top strands, whispering forgiveness and calming words, rocking him gently while he let the tears and demons go.

Countless minutes it went on, but eventually the racking sobs gave way to sniffles, then to Blaine's nose and lips teasing a trail from the divot at the hollow of Wags's throat to the underside of his chin.

"Blaine..."

"I owe—"

Wags drew back and cupped his face, thumbs over his lips. "You don't owe me anything. You only owe yourself a chance."

"I'm taking that chance," Blaine whispered against the pads of his thumbs. "With you." And then he flicked his tongue out, causing Wags to gasp and tremble with barely contained desire, giving Blaine an opening to wrap his lips around the tips of his thumbs and suck.

Wags groaned. Mentally begged his cock not to harden so fast. To give him a chance to do the right thing. "I'm not worth it. You don't kn—"

"I know enough." Blaine rose onto his knees and threw one leg across Wags's lap, straddling him and taking his face in his hands, the same way Wags had done to him. "You're a good man, Theodore Wagner, and tonight I need to forget all this before it becomes my life for the next however many months it takes to make sure my father rots in jail."

Determination shone through the leftover tears in his eyes, and Wags's admiration for the man in his lap swelled. He covered Blaine's hands with his own. "You know, you're incredible."

Blaine grinned. "Let me show you how incredible."

"I don't want to take advantage."

That grin tipped into a smirk. "If that's what you think is going on here, you're not half as smart as I thought you were." He leaned forward, lips brushing over Wags's. "Trust me."

He had to, didn't he? Blaine was an adult who'd been through more than most people his age. And this past weekend, he had proven himself skilled and competent. He knew his own mind, and that mind, remarkably, had trusted him, was set on him, at least for tonight.

"I do." Wags surrendered on a moan, and Blaine struck, more gently than Wags had anticipated, his tongue gliding between his lips, his fingers into his hair, his body closer, a slow slide into the pleasure they'd both been chasing since their Friday night encounter.

They kissed for what felt like days, taking turns exploring, Blaine seemingly after every corner of his mouth, learning how much Wags loved the brush of tongues, and Wags learning that Blaine squirmed in his lap when he sucked and nipped on his bottom lip. Eager to feel more of his hard body, Wags coasted his hands down Blaine's sides and over his arse, hauling him closer.

"Fuck," Blaine cursed. "I want to rub my dick all over you, but I can feel yours beneath me, and all I want to do is ride it." He whined into the crook of Wags's neck as he struggled to do both. "We are wearing entirely too much clothing."

Wags laughed, the struggle real for him too. "I haven't had sex in over a year. I may come before we even get out of said clothing."

Blaine jerked back, holding his gaze, assessing the truth of his statement. He must have liked what he saw because he threw back his head and laughed. Wags's cheeks heated, but the truth was the truth. And he was less bothered by the laughter when it sounded equal parts charmed and amused. It eased the last of the tension and sadness from before. Brought them back to the alley, to the car, to the church office. Each time they'd been interrupted, but no more. Resolve shone in Blaine's dark eyes, all of it directed at Wags.

"I'm going to make a mess of you," Blaine declared.

Reluctantly letting go of Blaine but more than eager for what those words promised, Wags flicked open several more shirt buttons, then reclined onto his elbows, offering himself to the man still spread across his lap. "Do your worst."

Blaine's eyes blazed. "Jesus, fuck, you're hot." He

planted one hand on Wags's chest, fingers tangling in his chest hair, and reached down to his own fly with the other, unzipping his jeans and pulling out his thick cock. Wags thrust up, unable to stop the inevitable, and Blaine countered, dragging along the ridge of Wags's cock as he stroked himself. "That's it, baby. Give me something to ride."

Wags kept rolling his hips, watching raptly as Blaine stroked himself, cock rock-hard and glistening with precome. Wags licked his lips. "I want that inside me."

"Mouth or ass?"

"Arse," Wags didn't hesitate to answer, desire zipping down his spine, his hole clenching harder than it had in the car earlier.

Blaine's fist moved faster. "What if I come all over these fancy clothes first?"

"Yes," he groaned. He wanted that too, wanted that messy, complete and utter abandon. The clothes weren't his anyway.

"You gonna show up at the airport in come-crusted clothes?"

Shifting onto one elbow, Wags stretched his other arm down and covered Blaine's fist, stroking him together. "Yes." He thrust up, hard. "Come for me."

Blaine groaned and quaked atop him, warm come spurting between their fingers and over Wags's borrowed pants and shirt.

Inside his boxers too.

Blaine stared down at him with lust-drunk eyes. "Did you make a mess?"

In answer, Wags lifted his come-sticky hand to his mouth, sucking one finger at a time, then licking between the digits.

"Hotter still," Blaine hummed, then offered his own hand, which Wags cleaned greedily, watching Blaine's cock harden again with each lick.

His own too, remarkably.

"Let's make more of one," Blaine said with a grin before rising to his knees and shifting backward, taking Wags's pants and sticky boxers with him as he scooted off the end of the bed. "Ditch the shirt," he said. "And get a pillow under those hips."

His come-and-spit-slick fingers slipped a couple of times on the rest of the buttons, but by the time Blaine finished undressing himself and retrieving condoms and lube from his bag, Wags was naked, his hips elevated, all his junk on display.

To Blaine's delight, judging by the feral grin that lit his face. He climbed onto the bed between Wags's legs and, hands on the insides of his thighs, spread them wider, his mouth hovering above his groin, his warm breath utter torture. "Fuck, you're a mess already." He licked the left-over come from the crease of his thigh, and Wags moaned. Collapsed the rest of the way onto his back and arched his neck, digging his head into the pillows as he begged for more. Blaine licked up the other crease. "You taste fucking amazing too."

"Fuck, Blaine, please."

Still maddeningly avoiding his cock, Blaine trailed his tongue down the seam of his balls, along his taint, then around his rim, teasing his hole. "I've gotta get this good and ready first, and then I'm gonna take you rough." He shoved a finger inside him, the intrusion sudden and painful and perfect. "Like you want it."

"Yes." Wags bore down on the finger and repeated his plea. "More, please."

"Okay, Teddy, I've got you."

Wags trusted that he did, same as Blaine had trusted him earlier, and just as Wags had taken care of him then, gotten him out of that church alive and to safety, Blaine did the same for him now.

By finally taking his cock into his mouth, all the way to the back of his throat, and swallowing around the tip. Making Wags shout. Licking and sucking his length with zero restraint. Giving his balls attention too, rolling them in his mouth, then palming them. Teasing and stretching his hole, three slick fingers pounding inside him while he sucked his cock, setting a relentless pace until Wags came down his throat with another shout.

The next moment, Blaine flipped him, and having held in reserve a mouthful of come, coated Wags's already messy hole with it, then drove inside him, digging his fingers into his hips and riding him hard, the headboard making a steady, rapid *thump* against the wall. Blaine pulled out at the last second, ripping off the condom and covering his arse and lower back with come like he'd done his front.

He sank down onto him after, knees tucked against his sides, arms tucked under his pits, lips nuzzling behind his ear. "Was that everything you wanted?"

Wags sighed, into the mattress, into the mess, into the warmth and sense of home covering him. "Everything and more."

NINE

They made it to the airport on time, barely.

Wags in the borrowed dress clothes that were still damp from trying to rinse the come out of them. Blaine in the spare set of clothes the little devil had had in his bag. Wags's duffel, though, by some Mel miracle, had been waiting for him at the airport, so as soon as the plane reached cruising altitude, he slipped into the bathroom and changed. When he returned, Blaine was dozing in the seat next to his, his mother's diary open on his lap.

Unsurprising, as they'd been up most of the night—fucking, talking, fucking some more—before catching a few hours of sleep between sunrise and rushing out the door to the airport. Wags hadn't been so worn out since his first off-base weekend from the RAF.

Unsurprising, too, that once a groggy Blaine closed the diary and leaned against his side, the warmth reminding Wags of those peaceful, fucked-out early morning hours in each other's arms, he'd fallen asleep himself, an arm around Blaine's shoulders, his head resting atop his.

And slept soundly until the kindly steward with silver hair and a posh RP accent gently shook him and Blaine awake. "We're beginning our descent into San Diego, gentlemen. We'll be on the ground in twenty."

"Thank you," Wags said, straightening in his seat.

Blaine made no such attempt, leaning more heavily into Wags's side and lacing their fingers together, resting their joined hands on Wags's thigh.

Wags glanced over his head out the window at the sunny desert landscape that was slowly getting closer. "Do you like it here?" he asked Blaine.

"Not particularly."

"It's very sunny."

Blaine chuckled. "Says the Londoner."

"I like San Francisco better."

"So do I." He snuggled closer, and Wags couldn't help but smile.

Couldn't help but hope for that home he'd dreamed about. For Blaine in his bed there too. Last night had given him a glimpse into what that fantasy future might look like. But first, there was reality to deal with, and Blaine's would largely be dictated by what his mother had written in the book still resting in his lap. "Are you ready for what's about to happen?"

"I'm ready for it to be over, once and for all."

Wags dropped a kiss on his crown. "You're incredible."

"Already showed you that." Blaine tilted back his head, his smile and dark eyes soft. "Would like to again. Maybe in San Francisco, once I get out." He would likely do jail time for fraud and digital forgery, but his cooperation with the authorities would reduce his sentence. Eighteen months,

Mel had estimated. Maybe less, given he'd be in her employ after.

"Some people waiting for you in Fog City, I hear."

"Same folks waiting for you, I hear," Blaine returned. "They seem like good people."

"That's my impression too."

Blaine squeezed his hand, drawing his gaze from where it had wandered out the window again. "You didn't answer my question. Last night was incredible. I can do my time, see myself in San Francisco after, if I know more of those nights are waiting for me. With you, Teddy."

More of the fantasy came into focus, closer to reality. But one night versus a future…

"Are you sure? I'm old and come with more baggage than just that duffel," he said with a side-eye to the old military-issue bag in the corner.

Blaine laughed out loud. "You're talking to me about baggage."

"Point taken." Wags chuckled, then sobered. "But, Blaine, you barely know me."

"I'd like to get to know you better." He stretched up, lips against the hinge of his jaw. "I'm willing to take a chance on you."

Wags angled his face down, into the kiss waiting for him, toward a future, a home, and a man he also wanted to know better. "Then I'll be there to take a chance on you too."

EPILOGUE

Twelve months later…

Wags checked the time on his phone, half past four, half past time, then paced the length of his flat once more—from the little balcony at the back of the unit, through the compact living-and-dining area, down the long, narrow hallway, past the bedroom with the secondhand furniture he'd bought and the office with the setup that had cost far more, even with the hacker friends and family discount. At the front door, he pulled back the gauzy material that covered the window, expecting an empty landing.

And finding Blaine instead.

"Fucking finally," he said, wrenching the door open.

"Press complications," Blaine replied. "Had to take the long way."

Wags had wanted to pick Blaine up from the detention facility, but expecting that at least a few reporters would want a comment from Blaine on his father's life sentence, Mel had insisted on doing the honors, on working her connections if a covert exit became necessary. Which it sounded like it had.

"You gonna invite me in?" Blaine said with a smirk, but the devilish grin was belied by the hope and nervousness in his eyes.

Wags was sure Blaine glimpsed the same in his. "It feels like I've been waiting forever." Since the day Mel had met them at the bottom of the private jet's stairs with Marsh, who'd taken Blaine back into custody. Wags had visited with him, but they'd rarely been alone, and never in their own space.

He opened the door wider, gesturing Blaine inside.

Blaine dropped his bag in the tiny foyer, a hand searing across Wags's chest before he drifted down the hallway, peeking into the bedroom, then freezing over the threshold to the office, whistling low. He grinned over his shoulder, blinding, and Wags almost missed his words. "Is this all for me?"

"For us." He stepped behind Blaine and looped an arm around his waist. "Jax said it would have whatever you need so you can do whatever you're going to do for Redemption. And it's built for what I need to do for them too."

Blaine sighed and melted back against him, his content- ment bleeding into Wags, filling the emptiness that had lingered the past twelve months. He'd been building a life here in San Francisco, but a crucial part of it had been on the periphery, updated but not fully present.

Until now.

He kissed Blaine's temple. "Got an even better view to show you."

"Of you naked, I hope."

Wags chuckled. He still wasn't sure what a young man as attractive and smart as Blaine saw in a middle-aged reno project like himself, but he'd stopped questioning it, Blaine's smile every time they'd visited convincing him this was real.

Blaine had also threatened to send his defense counsel, Helena Madigan, around to convince him, and after being in the Talley-Madigan orbit for the past couple of years, Wags knew Helena was second only to Mel on the Most Terrifying list—and it had nothing to with her courtroom persuasion skills.

"We'll get to the naked bit soon enough," Wags said, lowering his arm and snagging Blaine's hand. "But let me show you something first." He tugged Blaine farther into the flat and through the door onto the balcony.

If he'd thought Blaine content before, it was nothing compared to the total peace that washed over his face as the misty fog did the same, so thick today that it shrouded the Pyramid completely. Blaine squeezed his hand and leaned back against him. "It's fucking perfect."

Wags couldn't agree more, his London heart at peace here, even more so now that the man he loved was back in his arms. For good. "Welcome home." The home he'd always wanted, with the person he wanted to share it with. "If you're still willing to take that chance on me."

Blaine turned in his arms and brushed their lips together. "Thank you for taking one on me."

Wags had taken a lot of leaps in his life, but none had ever felt as right as catching the man who leapt into his arms, into his life, and carrying him into their home, into the future they were both willing to take a chance on, together.

For all the latest updates on new projects, sneak peeks, and more, including what's next for Redemption Inc., sign up for Layla's Newsletter.

Reviews are an invaluable tool when it comes to spreading the word about great reads. Please consider leaving an honest review for *The Bounty* on your favorite review site.

Thank you for reading!

ACKNOWLEDGMENTS

When Wags and Blaine first appeared on page in the Perfect Play series, I had no idea they were going to end up together. But as they continued to float around in this world, I started to noodle the possibility, and in the end, they were just what the other needed—a fresh start. And this short, spicy little story was just the Whiskey Verse fly-by I needed while I finished up some other projects.

Special thanks to EM Lindsey, who organized *A Safe Space*, the Read the Rainbow Charity Anthology where this story first appeared. And gave me the excuse to write it!

Thanks as well to Kim and Louise on the beta reads for this one, to Kelley York at Sleepy Fox Studio for another striking cover, to Keren Reed and Adam Mongaya on editing, and to Kate on graphics.

Finally, readers, thank you continued to love and enjoy the Whiskey Verse. Plenty more to come!

ALSO BY LAYLA REYNE

For the most up-to-date list of titles and a helpful reading order, please visit www.laylareyne.com.

Agents Irish and Whiskey:

Single Malt

Cask Strength

Barrel Proof

Tequila Sunrise

Blended Whiskey

Angel's Share

Trouble Brewing:

Imperial Stout

Craft Brew

Noble Hops

Final Gravity

Fog City:

Prince of Killers

King Slayer

A New Empire

Queen's Ransom

Silent Knight

What We May Be

Perfect Play:

Dead Draw

Bad Bishop

King Hunt

Best Play

Redemption Inc:

The Accidental

The Bounty

The Martyr

The Boss

Soul to Find:

Icarus and the Devil

Jason and the Storm

Paris and the Reaper

Atlas and the Traitor

Table for Two:

The Last Drop

Dine With Me

Blue Plate Special

Over a Barrel

Changing Lanes:

Relay

Medley

Freestyle

ABOUT THE AUTHOR

Layla Reyne is the author of *What We May Be* and the *Agents Irish and Whiskey, Fog City,* and *Perfect Play* series. She writes sexy, intense LGBTQIA+ romance featuring competent adults in kitchens, sports arenas, car chases, and other high-stakes situations. Whether it's adrenaline-fueled suspense, rival athletes, vampires and shifters, or love mixed with mouth-watering foodie goodness, queer folks finding happily-ever-afters is guaranteed.

You can find Layla online at laylareyne.com and at the following sites:

bookbub.com/authors/layla-reyne

facebook.com/laylareyne

instagram.com/laylareyne

tiktok.com/@laylareyne

bsky.app/profile/laylareyne